SCARE SCHOOL
~Diaries~

Welcome to Scare School

Julien  217 Grade 2

# Welcome to Scare School

BY JARRETT LERNER

## ALADDIN
New York  London  Toronto  Sydney  New Delhi

# For all of the fearless school librarians

ALADDIN
An imprint of Simon & Schuster Children's Publishing Division
1230 Avenue of the Americas, New York, New York 10020
First Aladdin paperback edition July 2024
Copyright © 2024 by Jarrett Lerner
Also available in an Aladdin hardcover edition.
All rights reserved, including the right of reproduction in whole or in part in any form.
ALADDIN and related logo are registered trademarks of Simon & Schuster, LLC.
Simon & Schuster: Celebrating 100 Years of Publishing in 2024
For information about special discounts for bulk purchases, please contact Simon & Schuster Special Sales at 1-866-506-1949 or business@simonandschuster.com.
The Simon & Schuster Speakers Bureau can bring authors to your live event.
For more information or to book an event contact the Simon & Schuster Speakers Bureau at 1-866-248-3049 or visit our website at www.simonspeakers.com.
Designed by Irene Vandervoort
The illustrations for this book were rendered digitally.
The text of this book was set in Scare School Thick.
Manufactured in the United States of America 1224 BID
4 6 8 10 9 7 5
Library of Congress Cataloging-in-Publication Data
Names: Lerner, Jarrett, author, illustrator.
Title: Welcome to scare school / by Jarrett Lerner ; illustrated by Jarrett Lerner.
Description: First Aladdin hardcover edition. | New York : Aladdin, 2024. |
Series: The scare school diaries ; 1 | Audience: Ages 5 to 8. |
Summary: Bash, a young ghost who has never been good at scaring people, is nervous about his first day at scare school, where he will learn to master the necessary skills to become a successful ghost.
Identifiers: LCCN 2023050954 (print) | LCCN 2023050955 (ebook) |
ISBN 9781665922098 (hc) | ISBN 9781665922081 (pbk) |
ISBN 9781665922104 (ebook)
Subjects: LCSH: Ghost stories. | Fear of failure—Juvenile fiction. |
Schools—Juvenile fiction. | CYAC: Ghosts—Fiction. | Fear—Fiction. |
First day of school—Fiction. | Schools—Fiction. | LCGFT: School fiction.
Classification: LCC PZ7.1.L4685 We 2024 (print) | LCC PZ7.1.L4685 (ebook) |
DDC 813.73 [Fic]—dc23/eng/20231120
LC record available at https://lccn.loc.gov/2023050954
LC ebook record available at https://lccn.loc.gov/2023050955

# PRIVATE

Do NOT turn another page . . .

# . . .OR ELSE!

**Student:** Bash (ghost)
**Homeroom:** Graves

| Period | Class |
|--------|-------|
| 1 | Introduction to Scare Tactics with Ms. Graves |
| 2 | Cackles, Laughs, and other Sinister Sounds with Mr. Crane |
| 3 | Human Behavior with Headmaster Dave |
| 4 | Lunch with Captain Loosebeard |
| 5 | Advanced Creeping and Crawling with Prof. Snekk |
| 6 | Philosophy of Fear with Ms. Scully |
| 7 | Creature Intensive with Mr. Crane |

# Sunday

Tomorrow is my first day at Scare School. Dad's dropping me off in the morning. And since this is my TOTALLY PRIVATE notebook that no one else is going to read EVER, I guess I can say . . .

I'm kind of SCARED.

Which is kinda silly, I know. Kids go to Scare School to learn how to BE SCARY, not to BE SCARED.

But I can't help it. I've just never been very good at all the GHOST STUFF.

Dad says I'm just a late bloomer. He says I'll learn my skills in no time, and that being at Scare School will help. He says the teachers there are the best of the best, and that soon enough I'll be as scary a ghost as any. He also keeps talking about how I'm going to make SO MANY friends....

Dad

[Insert optimistic stuff here]

But I'm not so sure about all
that. And maybe the friend thing
especially. I haven't spent much
time around creatures my own
age. And every time I have? Well,
let's just say it never goes well.

Um, hi. Hello. H-hey.
My, uh, Bash is name.
No! I mean, name is
my—ugh! I BASH!

Dad also keeps bringing up my sister.

"Bella went to Scare School," he says. "She loved it!"

And yeah, I know. But that's because Bella is Bella.

Bella was passing through brick walls as a baby. She could go invisible for a whole day by the time she was four. (She used to do it all the time when she didn't want to play with me.) Sometimes I think Bella was born with so much talent, there was none left over for ME.

FAMILY TALENT

Bella's share →

← Bash's share

Another thing I'm kind of worried about is that I'm going to have a ROOMMATE. That means

I have to share a bedroom with somebody else FOR THE WHOLE ENTIRE YEAR! AND I DON'T EVEN GET TO PICK WHO IT'S GOING TO BE!

But I have one more night here at home with Dad. So for now, I'm just going to focus on that.

Last dinner at home with Dad (we ate all my favorite things)

Popsicles

pizza

peppers

(I just realized all my favorite foods start with the letter p. . . .)

# Monday

Well, I did it.

    I survived my very first day at Scare School!

    Obviously.

    If I'd gotten eaten by a snot monster or something, I wouldn't be here writing in my diary.

You don't have a light in here, do you?

Me

Anyway, it was a loooooooong day. So much happened! And I want to make sure to get it all down. I'm going to start at the very beginning so I don't forget a thing. . . .

Me and Dad on the way to Scare School . . .

Dad (super happy and excited)

Me (NOT super happy and excited)

my stuff

Dad flew me all the way up to Scare School's gigantic front door. And once we were right up next to it, I could hear stuff coming from behind it. All sorts of sounds.

First, I heard footsteps. FAST ones. Like someone was running.

But then the running stopped, and I heard something I didn't expect.

Laughter. A bunch of it. There was a group of creatures behind that door cracking up, having the time of their lives. And hearing that? Well, I'm not going to lie. I was still nervous. But I was also just the tiniest bit curious, too.

I didn't have long to think about that, though. It was time for Dad and me to say our goodbyes.

creak

Eek!

Before Dad left, he told me—again—that I was going to do great at Scare School. But this time, he also said that if I DIDN'T do so great, it was okay. He'd still love me and be proud of me.

Then he said,

See you in a couple of weeks!

And just like that. Like it was no big deal!

The truth, though, is that I've never been away from Dad for two whole weeks before. I've never been away from Dad EVER. This is my first time sleeping away from home — and I've got to do it for ELEVEN nights in a row!

TODAY

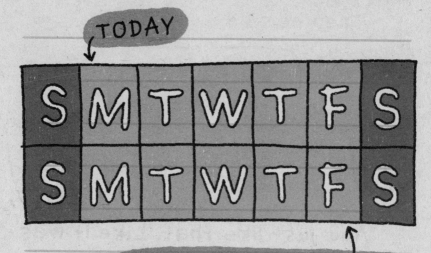

WHEN I SEE DAD AGAIN!

Classes at Scare School are broken up into sessions. Each session is two weeks long. At the end of each session, students get to go home and spend the weekend with their families. Unless they've been eaten by a snot monster. Then I guess they have to go to the snot monster's house for the weekend. . . .

Mommy!

Me

Anyway, pretty much as soon as I flew through the front door of the school—before I even really got a chance to look around—the day started.

Welcome to your orientation!

"Orientation," I found out, is just a fancy word for a day when you learn everything you need to know about a place and how it works. We were given our class schedules, then taken on a tour of the school. That actually took up most of the day, because halfway through the tour, Headmaster Dave misplaced his body. (We eventually found it in the library.)

We spent the rest of the day hanging out in the cafeteria, just getting to know all our teachers and classmates.

First: The Teachers!

**HEADMASTER DAVE** — Actually headless. Always happy and excited. Laughs for no apparent reason.

**MR. CRANE** — Never happy or excited. Probably has never laughed. Since he's also a ghost, I have to do my Creature Intensive with him. Bummer . . .

**MS. GRAVES** — My home-room teacher. She's got a big bowl of candy in her room, so she can't be THAT bad. Right?!

**PROFESSOR SNEKK** — Might even be more serious than Mr. Crane. I'm pretty nervous about class with him.

**CAPTAIN LOOSEBEARD** — The school cook. Seems super nice. Keeps talking about some dish he calls the "Bean Surprise."

**MS. SCULLY** — Also seems nice. She runs the library, and said we can check out as many books at a time as we want. Score!

## And Now: The Students!

**ITSY** — Sooo nice. Also FUNNY. I was next to her for most of orientation.

**VLAD + VICKY** — Sooo NOT nice. I stayed as far away from them as I could, but kept hearing them making jokes about everybody.

**WES** — A werewolf. Mostly kept to himself. But had a notebook he was drawing in. Maybe he'd want to draw with me?

24

MIMI — A snot monster! The first one I've ever seen in real life. They're not as scary as I thought they'd be. Or maybe it's just that Mimi doesn't seem all that scary?

ZARA — A zombie. First one of those I've seen in real life, too. Didn't get a chance to talk to her much.

MUMFORD — He talked to me a whole bunch, but I couldn't understand him through all his wrappings.

BATSLEE — ??? He slept through most of orientation.

Getting to know everyone was actually kind of . . . fun. I was nervous that I wouldn't know what to say to the other kids. But pretty much as soon as we all started talking, I forgot all about being nervous. It went fine. Great, even.

Wes likes to draw too! He's REALLY GOOD.

Snot monsters have a sense of humor!

Knock, knock ...

Eventually, we had dinner. (It was really good!) And then, just as we were finishing our desserts, Captain Loosebeard announced that it was time to get our roommate assignments. When I heard THAT, all the nervousness I'd stopped feeling came rushing back....

29

Can you believe it?!

I was so relieved.

Because if I'd been able to choose my own roommate, I definitely would've picked Itsy.

When we got to our room, I made my bed and Itsy spun herself a big, cozy web. Then she turned to me and said, "Hey, Bash? I'm glad we're roommates. I was hoping we'd be."

Really?

Really.

What a day. Like I said, it was a loooooooooong one. But also a good one. Which I hadn't been expecting.

It's got me thinking.... Maybe my time here at Scare School won't be so bad after all.

Though I guess I'll find out tomorrow. Because today was just orientation. Tomorrow is my first real day of classes.

# Tuesday

Today was my first day of actual classes.

It was...

Well, let's just say that it could've gone better. MUCH better.

But I do have one GOOD thing to report about my classes, and that's that Itsy is in almost all of them. And that made the day WAY better than it would've been otherwise.

Anyway, here are the highlights from my morning classes....

FIRST PERIOD

The unseen is often scarier than the seen. Which is why it's important for all of you to learn how to hide.

Aw, man. I've never been good at hiding . . .

Are you any good at it, Itsy?

Itsy?

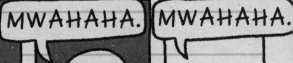

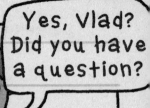
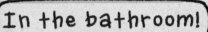

Fourth period, we have lunch.

It couldn't come soon enough!

At the start of the period, Captain Loosebeard went around with a big cart full of our food options for the day. He tried to get everyone to take some of his Bean Surprise. But it looked a little ... weird. It also had a funky smell. More like socks than beans.

I went with a grilled cheese.
JUST a grilled cheese. Batslee was
actually the only kid brave enough
to try the Bean Surprise.

Not bad.

Lunch was over way too soon.
And then it was time for the rest
of the day's classes. . . .

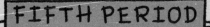

FIFTH PERIOD

Snekk snekk snekk snekk-snekk snekk SNEKK snekk snekk.

Are we supposed to be able to speak Snake?

I don't think so....

Snekk snekk, snekk SNEKK!

Snekk-snekk-snekk, snekk-snekk.

Seventh period I have my Creature Intensive with Mr. Crane. And since I'm the only ghost here at Scare School right now, it means it's JUST me and Mr. Crane. The class is supposed to help get me better at my "special creature skills," which are all the things that only ghosts can do.

MOST ghosts, I mean. Ones who are ACTUALLY good at ghost stuff.

After classes, Itsy and I hung out in our room. We did a little decorating, then Itsy showed me her books. And guess what? Half of them were comics! She even had a couple that I've got back at home too.

We talked about comics, and then, without realizing I was doing it, I asked if she wanted to see my sketchbook. As soon as I said it, I wished I hadn't. I've never shown ANYONE my sketch-book before. Not even Dad!

But then Itsy said . . .

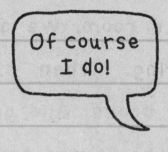

Of course
I do!

So I showed her.

And she seemed impressed!

These are
SO GOOD.

Then she said, "Hey! We should
make our own comic sometime."

I got excited about that.

We got right to it, even though we only had a little time left before dinner. But we already got a ton done. We made up a pair of superhero characters, and I did a few drawings of them. Itsy hung one up in our room!

After that, I was in a much better mood.

At dinner, right after we got our food, Ms. Scully went around the cafeteria with a stack of mail. I wasn't expecting to get a letter, especially since I'd only been at Scare School for a day. But then Ms. Scully set an envelope down right in front of me.

to Bash

But I was even more surprised when I turned the envelope over and saw who the letter was from.

from Bella

BELLA?!

(my big sister)

(NOT my biggest fan)

When Bella is home, she usually does everything she can to avoid talking to me.

And here she was writing me a letter?

It doesn't make any sense!

The only thing I can think is that Dad swung by the house she haunts on his way back from dropping me off yesterday, and that he'd somehow convinced her to do it.

Anyway . . .

Here's what she said:

Hey, little bro. I just got this new typewriter, so I figured I might as well write a letter and try it out.

I hope you're liking school all right. If you're not, you'll get used to it. And, hey — don't compare yourself to me. No one's as awesome as I am. So, you know, don't be too hard on yourself. Mr. Crane will be plenty hard on you as it is. LOL.

You can write me back if you feel like it. Or not. I don't care.

— Bella

I was still trying to wrap my head around the fact that MY SISTER had sent ME a letter when Headmaster Dave went up to the front of the cafeteria and cleared his throat.

He said that he hoped we all had a wonderful first day of classes. Then he said that he wanted to talk to all of us about our Creature Intensives.

I'd really rather not. . . .

Headmaster Dave told us that our Creature Intensives were to help us prepare for something called the C.A.T., which stood for the Creature Aptitude Test. I guess every student has to take a version of the test at the end of next week. In order to PASS the test, you have to prove that you can perform at least TWO of your special creature skills.

All of which is frightening enough.

But wait!

Because this is the REALLY SCARY part...

If you don't pass your test, YOU GET KICKED OUT OF SCARE SCHOOL!

Headmaster Dave didn't put it like that. He said something like, "Students who fail to pass their examination will not be eligible to enroll in any subsequent Scare School sessions," but that amounts to the same thing.

And I know, I know—just a couple of days ago, I didn't even

want to come to Scare School in the first place. But now that I'm here . . . I kind of like it. The classes are tough, sure. But I made a friend! And I'm pretty sure I might make a few more.

Itsy Mimi Batslee Wes

I don't want to get kicked out of Scare School.

Which means I've got to get better at being a ghost. FAST.

# SKILL CHART

| ghost skills | MY skills |
|---|---|
| "PASSING"— moving quickly and smoothly through solid objects | NONE— I can barely pass through a blanket |
| INVISIBILITY— instantly disappearing and staying "gone" as long as you want | Yeah, right. I've never even made myself TRANSLUCENT. |
| FLYING — ghosts must be fast and flexible, yet careful, flyers | I'm actually an okay flyer. Not GREAT. But okay. |

# Wednesday

Today, all anyone could talk about was THE TEST.

I tried to figure out if anyone else was as nervous about their test as I was about mine.

Vlad

Vicky

This test thing is going to be a CINCH!

I can do this all day—AND night!

Batslee

Yep, it seems like I'm the only one who has anything to worry about. How did everyone else get so good at their special creature skills?

Maybe it's because they really ARE special—and because I'm NOT. This sad, sorry fact was proven about a billion times today during my Creature Intensive with Mr. Crane. We spent all class working on passing. I couldn't even get myself all the way through a bedsheet....

When he saw that, Mr. Crane did NOT look pleased.

But, to be fair, I'm not sure Mr. Crane can even make any expression besides THIS one:

After the day's classes ended, Itsy and I hung out in our room again. As soon as we got there, she pulled out this piece of paper and hung it up on the wall, not far from where we'd put my Ghost Guy and Super Spider drawing.

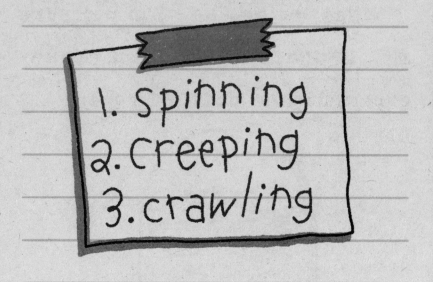

1. spinning
2. creeping
3. crawling

It only took me a second to realize what these were. Spider skills. The ones Itsy was going to have to perform during her version of the test.

Then she said, "Ready?"

But Itsy didn't even wait for me to answer. By the time I turned around, she'd already swung into action.

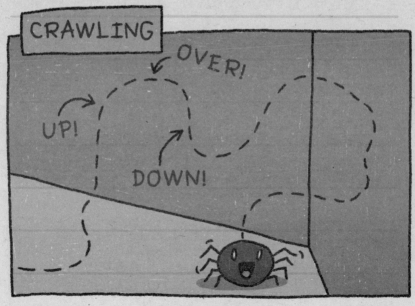

I told Itsy she was great. And I meant it. And I was really happy for her. She was going to pass her test—no question about it. But I think she could tell something was up with me.

Bash ... What's wrong?

And I just couldn't help it. . . .

Then Itsy said something amazing:

"But, Bash—the test isn't until the end of next week. We have plenty of time to get you ready for it!"

Friends are THE BEST.

# Thursday

Itsy and I had our first training session right after classes today. She said the first thing we had to do was get a sense of where I was with each of my skills. It was important to know just how much work we had to do.

That made sense. And so, even though I was very much NOT happy about it, I showed Itsy....

Here goes nothing.*

*Actually everything.

I started with flying, since that's what I'm best at.

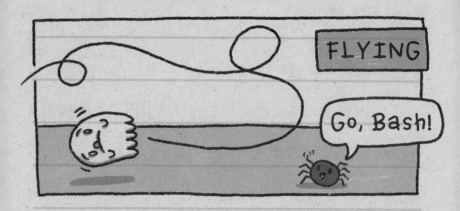

But things went downhill from there....

I know Itsy was just trying to be nice. I heard her compliment— but I also heard what she WASN'T saying. Which was: "And you're the OPPOSITE of great at your other two skills."

# Friday

No training session with Itsy today. She said she had to go to the library to read up on "ghost stuff."

I didn't know what to do, so I ended up writing a letter to Bella.

Hi!

A typewriter?! That's cool. I bet the typing sounds really creep out the family whose house you're haunting.

How is that, by the way? Are you having fun? Dad said he might visit you. Did he do that yet?

Don't worry. I'm definitely not going to compare myself to you. I know I'm not as good at being a ghost as you are. I'm so not good at it, actually, that I'm pretty sure I'm going to fail my test and...

...get kicked out of Scare School. So maybe I'll come visit you along with Dad, if he hasn't gone already.

Anyway. Thanks for writing to me. Or TYPING to me, I guess. It was... nice.

— Bash

P.S. Ms. Scully told me to tell you that she sends her best.

"ollo"

I didn't see Itsy again until dinner. And I was going to ask her if she'd learned anything useful at the library, but then . . . well, we got a little distracted.

Captain Loosebeard's Bean Surprise

Batslee . . . Do you think you should be eating so much of that?

What do you mean? It's DELICIOUS!

NOM!
NOM!
NOM!

TWENTY MINUTES LATER . . . .

in the hall, going to class

Ugh. I don't feel so good. . . .

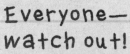

# Saturday

At Scare School, students get the weekends off. Some of the teachers set up activities that kids can take part in if they want. And some of them actually sounded kind of cool, like exploring the nearby forest or playing a big game of hide-and-seek. But there was only one activity I was really allowed to do today: training for my test with Itsy.

We started first thing in the morning, right after breakfast.

And Itsy was PREPARED.

She had all sorts of ideas for
how to help me improve my skills.

I wanted it to work. OBVIOUSLY.

I mean, Itsy had already put so

much time and effort into helping me. And if it didn't work, I knew she'd probably be disappointed. And having Mr. Crane be disappointed in me was one thing. But Itsy? I don't think I could take HER being disappointed in me. (It was already bad enough with just ME being disappointed in me.)

Unfortunately, watching Itsy swing back and forth wasn't making me feel invisible. The only thing it was making me feel was . . .

# SICK.

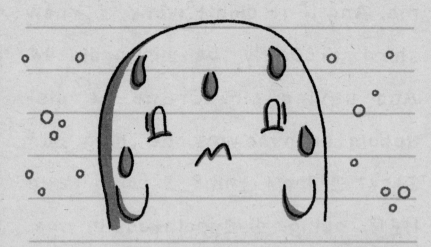

But I hadn't REALLY turned invisible.

I'd just had to rush out of the room and down the hall to the bathroom.

Because, well...

# Sunday

After yesterday's disaster, I kind of thought Itsy might give up on helping me. But after spending the morning back in the library (while I found a mirror and worked on my invisibility), she showed up to lunch with a brand-new idea.

"By the end of the day," she told me, "you're going to be the best ghost in the history of Scare School."

"Yeah?" I asked her, thinking that title probably belonged to Bella.

Itsy nodded confidently.

And I have to admit, it was nice to see her so certain about it. It made me feel like maybe Itsy was right. Maybe she really HAD figured out a foolproof way to help me improve my skills. I mean, if ANYONE could do it, I bet it'd be Itsy. She's pretty much a GENIUS.

So I said, "Okay! What are we going to do?"

Itsy grinned. "We're going to SCARE you!"

I felt so bad. For Itsy, mostly.
She was trying so hard to help
me. But it seemed I was un-helpable.
And then, as if the moment wasn't
bad enough. . . .

# Wednesday

Well, here we are.

The test is in just TWO DAYS. We've spent a lot of our class time practicing and preparing. But even when we're NOT focusing on the test, I can't seem to focus on anything else. . . .

Even though there's probably no use, Itsy and I spent the past couple days training some more. She refuses to give up. And I guess I HAVE gotten SLIGHTY better at one of my skills: invisibility.

But I still don't think I'm good enough for Mr. Crane.

And when it comes to passing? The situation there couldn't be worse. I think I've smashed into every single wall at Scare School.

Itsy is still as positive as ever, though. She keeps saying she believes in me. That she KNOWS I can—and WILL—pass my test.

But the thing is, I don't even believe in me. I don't think I can do it.

We'll find out soon enough. . . .

# Thursday

The test is TOMORROW.

So today, I said my goodbyes.

Goodbye, spot outside the lunchroom where someone spilled some of Captain Loosebeard's Bean Surprise and it burned a hole in the concrete floor. . . .

I was just about done when I heard something.

Heh-heh-heh.

I recognized Vlad's laugh. And I could only assume that he and his sister were up to something.

I was about to turn around to get out of there—I didn't want any part of whatever those vampires were doing.

But then I heard something else.

No! Don't!

It was ITSY.

And hearing her like that, all scared and in distress—I knew I couldn't just LEAVE her. I had to DO something. And RIGHT AWAY.

But what, I wondered, could I do?

little old me

I had no clue. But I got moving anyway, flying in the direction Vlad's laughter and Itsy's scream had come from.

The voices got louder the farther I flew down the hallway. But I still couldn't see Vlad, Vicky, or Itsy anywhere.

Finally, I got to the very end of the hall—to the very last classroom. I knew they all had to be inside.

But the door that led to the classroom—it was on the opposite side. To get to it I'd have to fly halfway around the school.

It would take me too long to fly all that way. Itsy needed me NOW. If I wanted to help her— and duh, I DID—I was going to have to pass through the wall!

I glared at the thing, then shut my eyes and tried to pretend that I wasn't just little old Bash, the world's worst, LEAST-special ghost. I tried to convince myself that I was HIM:

GHOST GUY

Then I flew into action.

And guess what?

I actually made it through the wall.

Some of it, at least.

Vlad and Vicky laughed so hard at me, they forgot all about what they'd been doing to Itsy. Soon enough, tears were streaming down Vlad's face. And he only

STOPPED laughing to say that he'd better go find a bathroom before he peed he pants. After which he and his sister finally wandered off, cracking up all over again.

Eventually, Itsy swung over and helped me get unstuck from the wall.

I felt terrible. I'd tried to help my friend, and not only had I failed miserably, I'd made a huge fool of myself in the process. But Itsy didn't seem to think so.

Itsy explained that if I hadn't gotten stuck in the wall and distracted them, they would've gone right on pulling at her legs.

Which I guess, technically, is true.

But it didn't make me feel any better.

Because if I can't even pass through a wall to save my friend, there's no way I'm going to be able to do it for the test.

Bash —

Sorry if it took me a while
to write back. I mean TYPE
back. Ha.

It's been busy around here.
The family who lives in the
house I'm haunting had a
bunch of people staying with
them, so I've been scaring
pretty much nonstop — mostly
when they're on the toilet.

To answer your question
about all that: It's good
here, but I don't plan to be
here forever. It's just not
challenging enough. Someday,
I hope I'll get a job
haunting a whole hotel or

something. We'll see.

Did you have your test yet? If you did, and it didn't go so well, don't worry. At least not too much. You can always get a job haunting a closet or something. Or maybe just a single drawer of a dresser. Or one of those things — what's it called? Oh yeah, right: a PORTA-POTTY!

Okay, I gotta go, little bro. Smell ya later!

— Bella

P.S. Tell Ms. Scully I said thanks!

# Friday

Most days I don't write in my diary first thing in the morning. I almost always wait until the very end of the day. But I didn't sleep well last night, and woke up super early. Everyone's still asleep. Even Itsy, who likes to get up early and read a bit before classes start in the morning.

Anyway...

Today's the day.

In an hour or so, I'll be on my way to take...

THE TEST!!!

I'm still not feeling good about my chances of passing. (How could I?) But I'm going to try to enjoy what I know is probably going to be my very last day here at Scare School. Because there are things I'm really going to miss about this place.

Itsy, of course.

But also Mimi and Batslee.

And Wes! I feel like we could be great friends. We both really love to draw.

I'll also miss some of the

teachers. Especially Ms. Scully and Captain Loosebeard. They're hilarious!

And yeah, sure—there are plenty of things about Scare School that I definitely WON'T miss.

Like these two:

And him:

But when you stack all that good stuff up against the rest, it doesn't seem THAT bad. All in all, Scare School is an awesome place. And if this is it, if it turns out I'll only ever get to spend two weeks here? Well, I'm still glad I got to.

Itsy just tooted. And usually, that means she's about to wake up, so I guess I'd better get going.

If I can bring myself to do it, I'll come back later and tell you all about how the test went. . . .

Okay.

I'm back home. HOME home.

And I'm ready to tell you all about . . .

# THE TEST

But I probably better start right where I left off, with Itsy waking up. Because when she opened her eyes and saw that I was already awake, she didn't reach for her book and do her usual reading. Instead she swung over to me.

I was sure she was going to bring up the test. I mean, the thing was set to start in just thirty minutes!

But Itsy surprised me. She didn't say a word about the test. Instead she asked me if I wanted to work on our first comic. And that's what we did.

I was so glad that Itsy had suggested we do all THAT rather than just sit there and worry about the test. I was putting my papers and pencils away when Itsy said, "We'll finish it up next week."

And I think I've got an idea for what our SECOND issue could be!

Of course, it was pretty likely that I wouldn't BE there next week....

But I decided not to bring that up. I just told Itsy that I couldn't wait to hear all about her idea and get back to work.

After that, we left our room and made our way to the cafeteria. We usually started the school day in our homerooms. But there was NOTHING usual about this day.

By the time Itsy and I got to the cafeteria, everyone else was already there.

Or ALMOST everyone . . .

Eventually, the last stragglers

showed up. . . .

After that, Ms. Scully took

attendance.

Then Professor Snekk led us all back out into the hallway.

slither    slither    slither

From there, he led everyone down to the gym.

It's basically just a big open space, but today there were all kinds of things set up through-out it—things that I quickly realized had been put there as part of each student's version of the test.

Like, on one of the walls, there was this giant sheet of paper with all these circles on it.

This was a target and was there for Mimi. She was going to have to blast some snot at it, after which the teachers would grade her based on how much of the snot she got on the bull's-eye.

Not too far from that, there was this fancy gadget that had wires and knobs all over it, plus a big meter on the front.

I knew this was for Wes, since I'd seen a drawing of the thing in his sketchbook. The machine measured sound. As part of his test, Wes was going to stand next to it and howl his head off.

And then, across the gym from the target and the gadget, I saw a brick wall. Not a brick wall holding something up — just a plain old brick wall, standing there all by itself. And I knew that THAT was there for me. . . .

Before I could get myself too worked up, though, the testing began. Ms. Graves cleared her throat and called out,

First up: Zara!

Zara did AWESOME. I've seen grown-up zombies who can't shamble and groan half as good as she can.

BRAAAAAAAAINS!

Wes went next. And you wouldn't believe just how loud that shy, quiet kid can howl. (My ears are still sort of ringing.)

AWOOO!

After Wes was Batslee. He had to shut his eyes and fly through this obstacle course that the teachers had set up along the gym's ceiling. And Batslee—he CRUSHED it. He whistled through the whole entire thing!

Mimi went after Batslee. She roared so hard her bow popped off, and shot out snot with A-plus accuracy.

After that it was Mumford's turn. He had to navigate an obstacle course of his own (though his was on the ground), then answer a bunch of questions about riddles and curses (he got EVERY SINGLE ONE right).

And then Vicky and Vlad went. And while it seemed like Vicky could've passed her test in her sleep, Vlad actually had a lot of trouble. When he was done performing his skills, the teachers had a little private meeting in the corner of the gym. They talked for nearly ten minutes before finally coming back and announcing that Vlad had passed.

Itsy went second to last. And—no surprise there—she did INCREDIBLE.

Then, finally, it was my turn . . .

gulp.

Mr. Crane flew up to me and went over what I was supposed to do. "You will have three minutes to perform your three special creature skills," he said. "In order to obtain a passing grade on your test, you must prove proficient in at least two of those skills."

I nodded.

Then Mr. Crane said, "You may begin."

I took a deep breath. Then I gave myself a quick pep talk.

After that I got to work.

I decided to start with flying, since it was the skill that I was best at—and the only one I knew I could definitely do. I swooped all the way up to the ceiling, then did some loops and quick turns, followed by a super steep dive.

Mr. Crane watched it all with his usual expression.

You know the one. . . .

But when I swept by him on my way to the brick wall, I'm pretty sure I heard him say, "Excellent."

I didn't have any time to think about any of that, though. I only had a couple of minutes left—and I knew I'd probably need every second of them.

I flew up to the brick wall. And looking at it up close, knowing that I had to try to pass through it ... well, I felt TERRIFIED.

But then something kind of incredible happened.

First, I heard Itsy shout, "You got this, Bash!"

I turned to look, and saw that she was right at the front of the crowd of onlookers.

Behind her, Mimi was slapping her tentacles together, clapping for me. Next to HER was Ms. Scully, and SHE gave me a wink. And then Wes—he brought his fingers to his lips and gave a great big whistle.

Looking at them all, I had this thought. Or no, it was more than

just a thought. It was one of

those things. . . .

An epiphany!

Me, having an epiphany (which is a word I know thanks to Itsy!)

A couple of weeks ago, when

I'd first showed up at Scare

School, I'd been full of fear. But

since then, so much had changed.

And I'D changed, too. So, so much.

I'd made my first real friend—
and I was pretty sure she was
just as excited about me as I was
about her.

I'd also met a snot monster—
and she'd turned out to be the
kindest, sweetest creature ever.

I'd met a skeleton, too—and the worst thing she ever did was tell jokes so funny that your juice came squirting out of your nose.

HAHAHA!

I'd even met a couple of vampires. And yeah, they could be every bit as mean as they looked. But really, they're more ANNOYING than they are SCARY.

I thought all that, then turned back to the brick wall. And this time, looking at the thing—I didn't feel scared at all. Because, I mean, being scared of a brick wall? Now, that just seemed a little silly.

I smiled. And I'm pretty sure, if I'd had a chance, I would've started laughing. But before I could, Mr. Crane flew over to give me a little reminder.

The clock is ticking!

Whoops!

I took another breath—and
then I went for it.

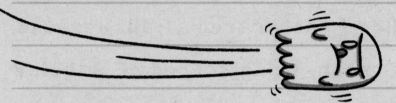

I flew full speed toward the
wall....

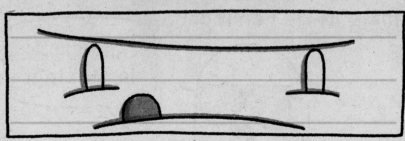

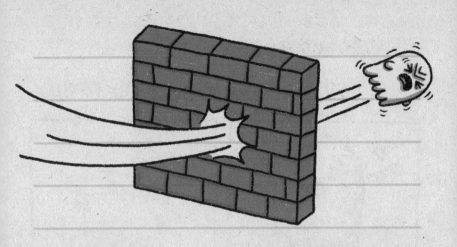

I did it.

I did it!

I DID IT!!!

But I didn't have much time to celebrate.

TEN! NINE! EIGHT! SEVEN!

Whoops again!

I still had one more skill to do.

Did I do it?

A part of me still can't believe that I actually passed the test. But another part of me—a part of me that, I think, keeps getting bigger and bigger—definitely CAN.

Maybe I'm not so bad at this whole ghost thing after all.

Congrats, Bash! I knew you could do it.

I'm back at home now, like I said, and I'm glad to be here. But I'm also glad that, in just a couple of days, I'll be heading back to Scare School. And seeing as I'm just about out of pages, it looks like I'm going to need to get another notebook!